Katie Finds a Job

by Fran Manushkin

illustrated by Tammie Lyon

PICTURE WINDOW BOOKS

a capstone imprint

Katie Woo is published by Picture Window Books,
A Capstone Imprint
1710 Roe Crest Drive
North Mankato, Minnesota 56003
www.capstonepub.com

Library of Congress Cataloging-in-Publication Data
Manushkin, Fran.
Katie finds a job / by Fran Manushkin; illustrated by Tammie Lyon.
p. cm. — (Katie Woo)
ISBN 978-1-4048-6513-6 (library binding)
ISBN 978-1-4048-6614-0 (paperback)
[1. Occupations—Fiction. 2. Schools—Fiction. 3. Chinese Americans—Fiction.]
I. Lyon, Tammie, ill. II. Title.
PZ7.M3195Kam 2011
[E]—dc22   2010030651

Summary: Katie must choose a job for a project at school.

Art Director: Kay Fraser
Graphic Designer: Emily Harris
Production Specialist: Michelle Biedscheid

Photo Credits
Fran Manushkin, pg. 26
Tammie Lyon, pg. 26

Printed in the United States of America,
003566

Table of Contents

Chapter 1
Looking for a Job

"I have to find a job,"

Katie told her mom.

"There's no hurry," her

mom said. "You have years

to think about it."

"I don't," sighed Katie. "I need a job by Friday. We are having Career Day at school. I need to talk about the job I want when I grow up."

Katie asked the bus driver,

"Do you like driving a bus?"

"Yes!" the driver said.

"I might like it, too," said

Katie. "Can I try driving?"

"I don't think so," the driver

said. "You're too young."

Pedro's dad

worked at a bank.

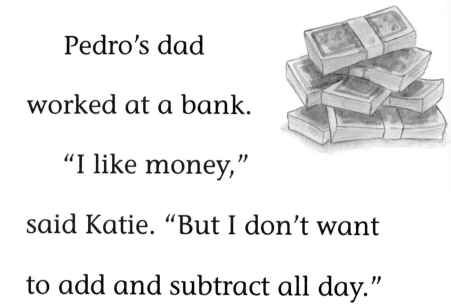

"I like money,"

said Katie. "But I don't want

to add and subtract all day."

Pedro's mom said, "Taking care of a new baby is a big job."

"That's for sure," Katie agreed. "I'm not ready to be a mom!"

"I like being a chef," said Katie's mom.

"I like to eat," Katie said. "But I don't want to cook all day."

Chapter 2
Helping Friends

"I love the sea and whales," said JoJo. "My job will be teaching people about them. But how can I do a great Career Day talk on whales?"

"I know how!" said Katie.

"We will make a giant

whale, and you can play a

CD of their songs. My dad

has one at home."

"That's terrific!" said JoJo.

"I'm going to

be a geologist,"

said Pedro. "I'm bringing lots

of rocks for my talk."

Katie shook her head.

"Pedro, you need more than

a pile of rocks."

"I have an idea," Katie

said. "Let's make a volcano."

She found a book that

showed how to do it.

"Wow!" shouted Pedro.

"My talk will be terrific!"

But Katie still did not

have a job.

"I can't decide," she said.

"I love to do a little bit of

everything."

Chapter 3

Career Day

Finally, it was Career Day.

JoJo's talk was splendid.

"Your whale songs added

so much," said Miss Winkle.

Pedro's volcano was exciting! "Well done!" said Miss Winkle.

The whole class clapped and cheered.

"Katie," said Miss Winkle, "it's time to tell us about your job."

Katie stood up. "I'm sorry," she said. "But I couldn't find one." She sat down again, looking sad.

"Wait a minute!" said

Pedro. "Katie did a great job

helping me. She showed me

how to build a volcano!"

"Katie helped me, too,"

said JoJo. "She gave me

terrific ideas! Katie's good at

telling people what to do."

"That's it!" Katie told Miss

Winkle. "I'll be the person

who tells people what to do!

Is that a job?"

"It is," said Miss
Winkle. "People who
solve problems are
called leaders."

"I'm a leader!" said Katie
proudly. "I'll go around
the world and fix every
problem!"

"That's a big job," Miss Winkle said. "Why don't you start with something smaller?"

"Okay," decided Katie, "I'll just be the president of the United States."

"Well," said Miss Winkle, "that's a big job, too. But if anyone can do it, it's you, Katie Woo!"

About the Author

Fran Manushkin is the author of many popular picture books, including *How Mama Brought the Spring; Baby, Come Out!; Latkes and Applesauce: A Hanukkah Story;* and *The Tushy Book.* There is a real Katie Woo — she's Fran's great-niece — but she never gets in half the trouble of the Katie Woo in the books. Fran writes on her beloved Mac computer in New York City, without the help of her two naughty cats, Gilda and Goldy.

About the Illustrator

Tammie Lyon began her love for drawing at a young age while sitting at the kitchen table with her dad. She continued her love of art and eventually attended the Columbus College of Art and Design, where she earned a bachelors degree in fine art. After a brief career as a professional ballet dancer, she decided to devote herself full time to illustration. Today she lives with her husband, Lee, in Cincinnati, Ohio. Her dogs, Gus and Dudley, keep her company as she works in her studio.

Glossary

career (kuh-RIHR)—the work or the series of jobs that a person has

chef (SHEF)—the main cook in a restaurant

geologist (jee-OL-uh-jist)—a person who studies the Earth's layers of soil and rocks

sighed (SYED)—breathed out deeply to express sadness or frustration

splendid (SPLEN-did)—very good or excellent

terrific (tuh-RIF-ik)—very good or wonderful

volcano (vol-KAY-noh)—a mountain with vents through which lava, ash, and gas erupt

Discussion Questions

1. Katie could not decide what job to choose for her Career Day. Have you ever had a hard time making a decision? What was it? How did you finally decide?

2. The book talks about several different jobs. Which of the jobs mentioned is the most interesting to you? Why?

3. If Katie Woo ran for president, would you vote for her? Why or why not?

FIND A JOB

Writing Prompts

1. What do you want to be when you grow up? Draw a picture of you doing your job. Then complete this sentence: I want to be a _____ because . . .

2. Katie wants to be the president of the United States. List three things she would do as president.

3. Make a poster for a pretend Career Day. Be sure to include a date and time, along with any other information students would need.

In this book, Katie explores a lot of different jobs. There are many kinds of workers. Think about all the people in your life. What jobs do they have? In your school alone there are teachers, lunchroom workers, custodians, and many more.

Here is a fun game to get you thinking about jobs. Play it with your friends or classmates.

Guess that Job!

* For two or more players

1. Choose one player to go first. That person should think of a job.

2. The other players ask yes-or-no questions to figure out what job has been picked. These are questions that can only be answered with "yes" or "no."

3. Whoever guesses the correct job gets to be the next person to choose a job.

Helpful Hints

• Ask a few questions to narrow down the type of job it may be. For example: Do people with this job help others? Do they make something?

• Some questions can be about where people work. Do they work outside? Do they work in an office? Or maybe a hospital?

• Another type of helpful question is about what they wear. Do they where a special uniform? Do they wear dressy clothes? Do they have a special hat?

• Some jobs use special tools or equipment. Do you use a computer at this job? Is there a special car or truck for this job?

Career
Day
Today!

THE FUN DOESN'T STOP HERE!

Discover more at www.capstonekids.com

- ♥ Videos & Contests
- ❀ Games & Puzzles
- ♥ Friends & Favorites
- ❀ Authors & Illustrators

Find cool websites and more books like this one at www.facthound.com. Just type in the Book ID: **9781404865136** and you're ready to go!